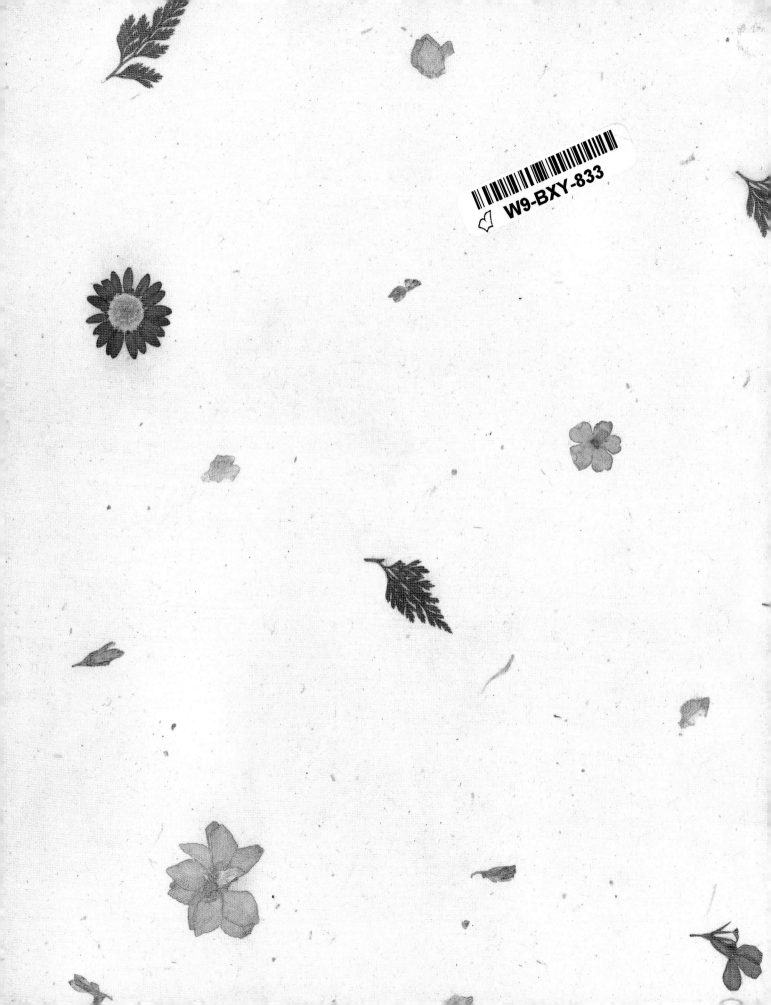

Harriet Ziefert

GRANDMA, IT'S FOR YOU!

ILLUSTRATIONS BY
Lauren Browne

BLUE APPLE BOOKS

For Jennifer
—H.Z.

For DEB
—L.B.

Text copyright © 2006 by Harriet Ziefert
Illustrations copyright © 2006 by Lauren Browne
All rights reserved
CIP Data is available.
Published in the United States 2006 by
Blue Apple Books
515 Valley Street, Maplewood, N.J. 07040
www.blueapplebooks.com
Distributed in the U.S. by Chronicle Books

First Edition
Printed in China

ISBN 10: 1-59354-109-0
ISBN 13: 978-1-59354-109-5

1 3 5 7 9 10 8 6 4 2

This is Lulu.
She wants to give her grandma
a really good present.

She'd like the present to be big.
She'd like the present to be beautiful.
She'd like the present to be the best present
her grandma has ever received.

Lulu asks,
"What should I make
for Grandma?"

Lulu's mommy is working.
She quickly answers,
"Lulu, Grandma will like whatever you give her."

Lulu gets dressed.
She tries on lots of outfits.

Finally she settles on one.

Now she is ready to make the biggest,
the best, and the most beautiful present
her grandma has ever seen.

Lulu likes clothes.
Lulu likes accessories.

Lulu knows her grandma
likes accessories, too.

So Lulu decides to make her grandma a hat—
a special hat decorated with all
of her grandmother's favorite things.

Lulu finds an old straw hat in her mommy's closet.
She takes it down.

The hat is plain.
But Lulu will make
it beautiful.

Lulu gets to work.

She collects flowers . . .

and leaves . . .

and even a few
bird feathers.

It's important
to have enough.

Lulu puts the flowers and leaves all around
the brim of the hat.

She carefully pokes the feathers
through the straw.

Then Lulu tries on the hat.
She is not happy. The hat is too plain!

Lulu runs to her room.

She finds a pink tutu . . .

some red ribbon . . .

and a necklace.

It's important to have enough.

Lulu decorates
the hat with a little
bit of everything.

Carefully, she tries on her creation.

Beautiful?

Beautiful.
But not beautiful enough.

The brim of the hat looks perfect.
But the top is still very plain.

Lulu adds a bird's nest,
and she's done.

Beautiful!

Lulu puts the hat on the kitchen table
and waits for her grandmother to arrive.

She's impatient.
She wants to give her grandmother the hat
and she doesn't want to wait another minute.

As soon as Grandma walks in,
Lulu grabs her arm and says,
"Grandma, look what I made for you!"

"Sit down, Grandma!"
Lulu proudly puts the hat on her grandmother's head.

Lulu's grandmother says,
"This is a fantastic hat ... created by Lulu!
You must have worked on it for a long time."

Grandma smiles.

Beautiful!

"Thank you for my one-of-a-kind hat.
You're my one-of-a-kind girl!

Now may I have a hello kiss?"